To Dad and Mom, Family, and Friends

www.mascotbooks.com

Ducks and Donuts

The illustrations are pen and ink, color pencils, watercolors

For more information, please contact:
Mascot Books
560 Herndon Parkway #120
Herndon, VA 20170
info@mascotbooks.com

Library of Congress Control Number: 2016915271

CPSIA Code: PRT1216A
ISBN-13: 978-1-68401-010-3

Printed in the United States

Ducks
and
Donuts

A Tale of Self-Reliance

Story and Pictures
by Robert DeNicola

Every day the ducks gathered outside the bake shop, captivated by the delicious aroma of cinnamon and spice. Zeff, a happy duck, a busy duck, was always last to arrive.

Every day at noon, the bakers came outside and fed the ducks their leftover cinnamon donuts.

Since Zeff was always last, there were never any donuts left for him. Sometimes a donut would float by, but who wants to eat a soggy donut? One night, Zeff decided he was going to be the first to arrive at the bake shop. He was finally going to taste a scrumptious cinnamon donut. That night, Zeff had big donut dreams.

In the morning when Zeff woke, he was surrounded by the saddest ducks.

"The bakers will not be coming today," the ducks quacked. For the first time in 50 years, the bake shop was closed.

"We don't know how we'll eat without those tasty cinnamon donuts."

"Well," Zeff cheerfully quacked, "there's this great pond full of fish you can catch."

"We haven't caught a fish in years! Some of us have never learned," the ducks replied.

"Let me show you what keeps me busy," quacked Zeff.

Zeff led the ducks out to the
middle of the great pond. Everyone
gathered around, and Zeff began to
show the ducks how to catch a fish.

With great ease, Zeff caught one
fish after another.

When it was the other ducks' turn, they were much too slow for the fast and slippery fish. Every time they attempted to catch one, they came up empty and gasping for air.

The hours passed, and a great hunger grew in their bellies. Some ducks wanted to give up. Some ducks grew scared, and others wanted to find a new bake shop.

Zeff quacked loudly, "Stop struggling! Be still and watch how the fish swim."

The fish swam up and down and wiggled all around.

By just watching the fish, the ducks forgot about their hunger. They forgot about finding another bake shop. But most of all, they forgot about giving up.

It took time, but eventually the once fast fish didn't seem so quick anymore.

Suddenly, a duck broke the water...

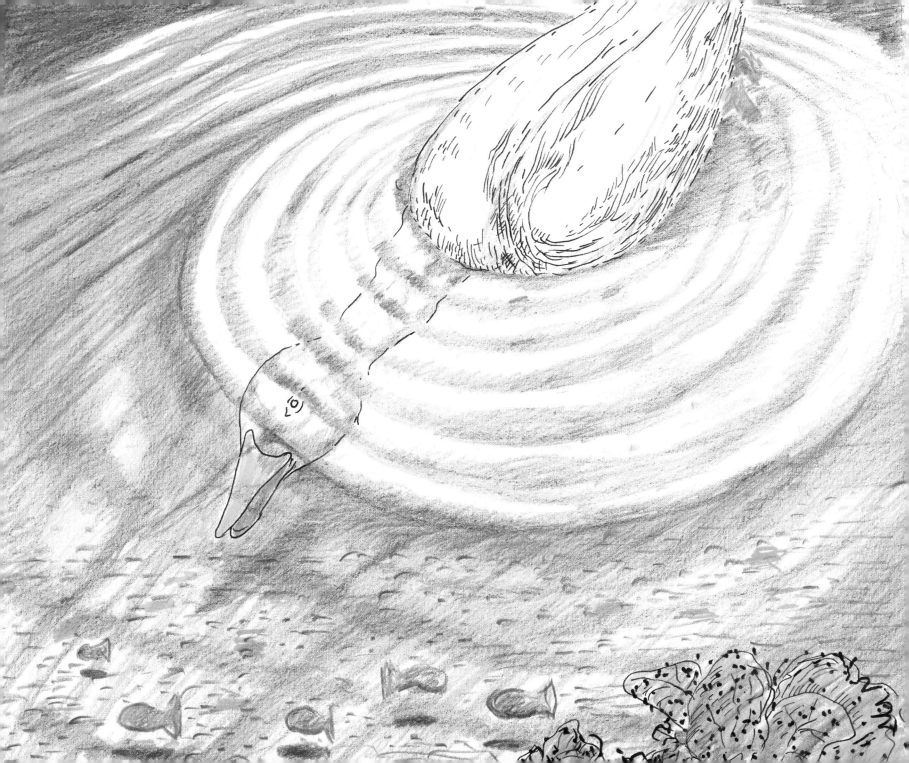

and caught a fish!

"That's it!" Zeff quacked. "You've got it!"

One by one, each duck triumphantly emerged with a fish.

It was a long day for the ducks, but they never went hungry again.

For Zeff, he never did get to taste a cinnamon donut, but he was perfectly fine with that.